Sniff

by
Lynne Hudson

Hello, my name is Scruffy,
and I've lost my blanket.

Where can it be?
It's snuggly and warm
and smells just like me.

I know, I'll sniff it out!

So I lift up my nose to sniff the air.

Sniff! Sniff! Sniff!

What's that smell on the ground – over there?

A cheesy, sweaty sock. YUK!

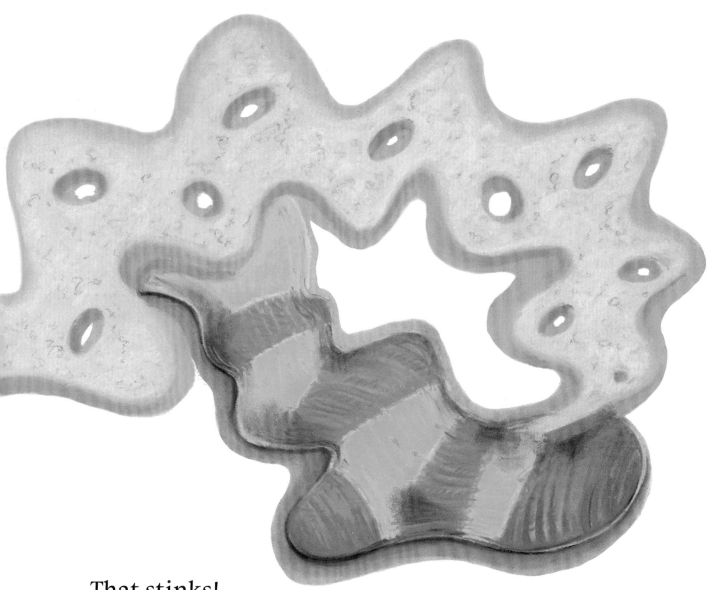

That stinks!

But it's better ahead;

I think I'll follow this nice smell instead.

The smell is so tempting –
rich, buttery and sweet.
My tummy is rumbling ...

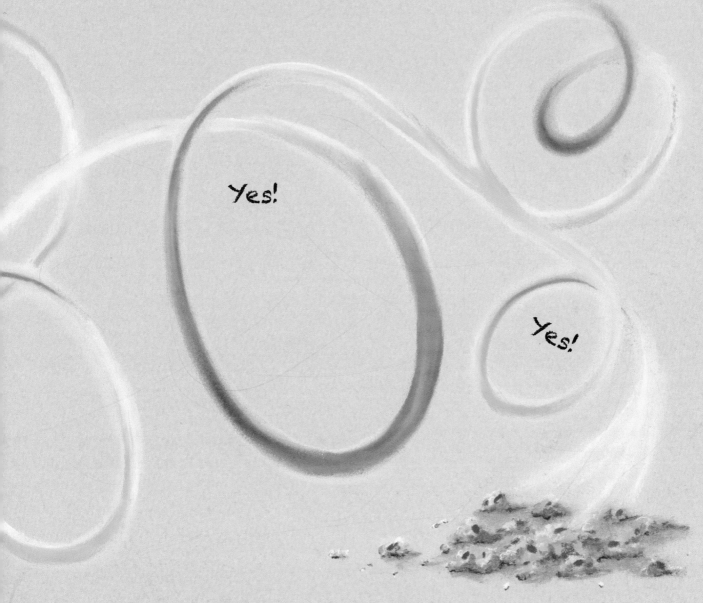

They tasted good, but I still haven't found my blanket.

I find more smells as I follow my nose –
the damp, mossy ground,
a bluebell and rose,
the smell of a rabbit
and a prickly hedgehog ...

... but they're not my blanket,
  and they don't smell of dog.

  So I sniff and I snuffle
  as I scurry around
  'til I smell something new –
  look what I've found!

Sniff! Sniff! Sniff!

There on a line
flapping high, all alone,
is a big chequered blanket,
which reminds me of home.

It's clean and it's fresh
and it's billowing and bright.
It looks like my blanket,
but ...

Sniff! Sniff! Sniff!

... it doesn't smell right.
So I'll grab it and pull it
and tug 'til it's free.

Then I'll rub and I'll roll ...

... 'til it smells just like me!

For Elloura and Lorelai

Published by
Hogs Back Books
The Stables
Down Place
Hogs Back
Guildford GU3 1DE
www.hogsbackbooks.com

Printed in Malta
ISBN: 978-1-907432-18-7
British Library Cataloguing-in-Publication Data.
A catalogue record for this book is available from the British Library.
1 3 5 4 2